CROC AND BIRD

For Luke

CROC AND BIRD
A HUTCHINSON BOOK 978 0 091 89332 3

Published in Great Britain by Hutchinson,
an imprint of Random House Children's Publishers UK
A Random House Group Company

This edition published 2012

3 5 7 9 10 8 6 4 2

Copyright © Alexis Deacon, 2012

RANDOM HOUSE CHILDREN'S PUBLISHERS UK
61–63 Uxbridge Road, London W5 5SA

www.randomhousechildrens.co.uk
www.randomhouse.co.uk

Addresses for companies within The Random House Group Limited can be found at: www.randomhouse.co.uk/offices.htm

THE RANDOM HOUSE GROUP Limited Reg. No. 954009

A CIP catalogue record for this book is available from the British Library.

Printed in China

The Random House Group Limited supports The Forest Stewardship Council® (FSC®), the leading international forest certification organisation.
Our books carrying the FSC label are printed on FSC® certified paper. FSC is the only forest certification scheme endorsed by the
leading environmental organisations, including Greenpeace. Our paper procurement policy can be found at www.randomhouse.co.uk/environment

FSC
www.fsc.org
MIX
Paper from
responsible sources
FSC® C104723

Loans are up to 28 days. Fines are charged if items are
not returned by the due date. Items can be renewed
at the Library, via the internet or by telephone up to
3 times. Items in demand will not be renewed.
Please use a bookmark

Check out our online catalogue to see what's in stock, or
to renew or reserve books.

www.birmingham.gov.uk/libcat

www.birmingham.gov.uk/libraries

CROC AND BIRD

ALEXIS DEACON

HUTCHINSON

Side by side on the sand sat two eggs.

A bird . . .   and a crocodile.

"Hello brother," said Bird.   "I'm hungry," said Crocodile.

"Open your mouth as
wide as you can and food
will come," said Bird.

So they waited . . .

and waited . . .

but food did not come.
"Perhaps I should go and
look for some," said Crocodile.

"I wonder what food looks like . . ."

"I don't know what we like,
so I've brought a selection,"
he said when he came back.

"Could you chew
it for me?"
asked Bird.

When they had finished,
they sat together on the sand,
looking at the world.
"I'm cold," said Crocodile.
"Me too," said Bird.

Then the sun rose.

"Look . . . it's beautiful,"
said Crocodile.
"I think we should sing
to it," said Bird.

"Singing makes me sleepy," said Crocodile,

and then he fell asleep.

When Crocodile woke up, Bird was sitting on something.
"Oooh," said Crocodile. "What is it?"

"It's our home," said Bird.

Days went by.

Crocodile and Bird grew big together.

They practised flying,
and they practised
lying like logs
in the water.

They practised
climbing,

and they
practised
dancing.

When the weather
was fine,
they basked
on the hot rocks.

When it was bad,
they fluffed up to
keep warm.
"I'm glad you're
my brother,"
said Crocodile.

Then one day
when they were
out hunting,
the river carried
them far away...

to a lake full of
crocodiles by a
forest full of birds.

They looked at them and they looked at each other.

"Oh," said Bird. "How silly we've been."
"We're not brothers at all," said Crocodile.
"I suppose we have to say goodbye," said Bird.
"Goodbye," said Crocodile.

Crocodile swam off to be with the crocodiles.
Bird flew off to be with the birds.

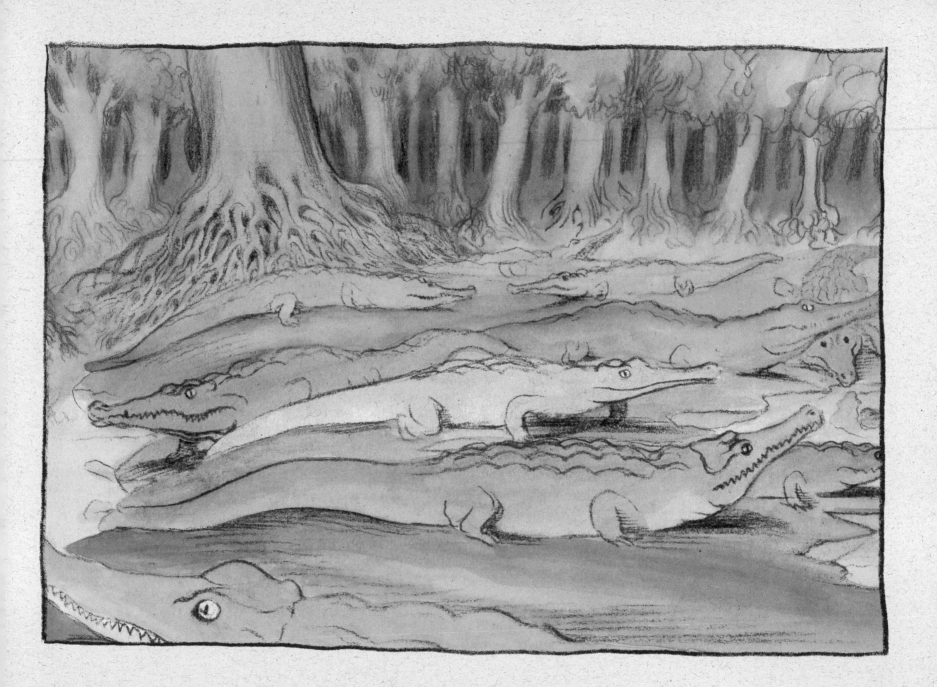

Next morning, Crocodile
greeted the sun with a song.
"Be quiet," said the crocodiles.

At lunch, Bird caught
a buffalo. "That's
disgusting," said the birds.

In the evening, Crocodile said, "I've built us a nest!" But no-one cared.

When it got dark, Bird flew away by himself. "Come back," called the other birds. "We don't fly at night."

Bird found Crocodile
perched in a tree.

"I couldn't sleep," said Bird.
"Me neither," said Crocodile.
"I missed you," said Bird.
"Me too," said Crocodile.

"Brother?" said Bird.
"Yes?" said Crocodile.

"Good night."